Teddy Discovers Color in the Woods

Dianne Shepherd Havard

Author and Illustrator

Dedication

To all my grandchildren

and to all your children and grandchildren,

may they enjoy all the fun that a walk in the woods can provide.

One of the things that makes Teddy and me glad

is to walk through the woods following my Dad.

This time we are looking for colors that I want to teach Teddy,

so that, when we start school, we will both be ready.

As we enter the woods, unseen by me,

Teddy's kerchief is loosened and caught by a tree.

We are so happy to be searching along

we do not even notice that the kerchief is gone.

In the woods, growing upward as far as we can see,

are Oak, Pine, and Magnolia trees.

Since we are both little and low to the ground,

many colored treasures by us can be found.

First, Teddy spotted moss way down low.

It was on the cool forest floor where it liked to grow.

It looked so inviting he said he would give it a test

and laid himself down on it to take a rest.

The moss was soft and such a bright green.

Teddy said it felt like a bed fit for a king.

This is the way Teddy and I like to play.

We let our imagination carry us away.

For nearby, like little stools, we saw white mushrooms circling around.

We thought it the perfect place for fairies to sit down.

There hidden in that bush is a little bird nest of brown.
It is made from sticks and looks like a woven crown.

Mama Bird has picked a perfect place to hide
her three little eggs that are nestled inside.

Teddy was distracted and did not get to see,

so, I showed him the outer covering of a nearby tree.

Brown is the color of the bark on this tall pine.

In it hides a worm on which the bird likes to dine.

Way up high, unseen by us,
are trumpet-shaped flowers waiting for the wind to gust.

Little yellow flowers that then float down from the vine
and look like gold on the ground, a surprise treasure to find.

Floating down and even bluer than the sky
is the lost feather of a bird that went flying by.

I tried to show Teddy the bird we call Blue Jay
but the bird had already flown away.

Just then, a black snake raced into Teddy's sight.

He jumped in my arms it gave him such a fright.

"Don't worry Teddy, he is just headed for under that wood

and he is the kind of snake that we call good."

The orange color we glimpse is a kumquat, little and round.

Dad carefully shook the tree, but one would not come down.

Since it is high in that spiny tree,

Dad must hold us up so that we can see.

Learning colors with Teddy is lots of fun,

but suddenly, a misty rain stops us before we are done.

Because of the rain we must turn around.

On our way out, we see the red color we have not yet found.

Finding the kerchief makes us glad,

but leaving the woods makes me a little sad.

I wanted to show Teddy so much more,

so many more colors out there to explore.

We are getting wet, so laughing, Teddy and I begin to run,

but, like quick summer showers, at the woods edge, out comes the sun.

Then, amazingly, to our surprise,

God unfolds a rainbow right before our eyes!

Red, orange, yellow, green, blue, indigo, and violet.

Some colors we have seen but violet not yet.

God's beautiful colors spread out in all their glory.

It is the perfect ending to our color story!

Made in the USA
Columbia, SC
17 November 2021

48929382R00018